Little Turtle
Turns the Tide

Lauren Davies
Illustrated By Nico Williams

Inspired by Bo Reef, my mini activist, the future is yours.
&
For Coco, my forever soul dog.
xx Mama

For Ruby and Lana x

Little Turtle Turns the Tide

ISBN: 978-0-9930383-5-8

Text copyright © Lauren Davies 2019
Illustrations copyright © Nico Williams 2019

Published by Orca Publications Ltd
Berry Road Studios
Berry Road
Newquay
TR7 1AT
UK
www.orcasurf.co.uk

Printed by Deltor Printing, Cornwall, on paper sourced from sustainable sources (FSC paper) using bio inks.

Little Turtle
Turns the Tide

Lauren Davies
Illustrated By Nico Williams

A baby turtle left his egg and crawled towards the sea.
It was his first adventure in the world of you and me!

He dreamed of bright blue water
and pods of happy whales,
who danced and sang beneath the waves
and leaped and splashed their tails.

Of coral, bright as rainbows
and sand as soft as snow.
Of multicoloured jellyfish
and angler fish that glow.

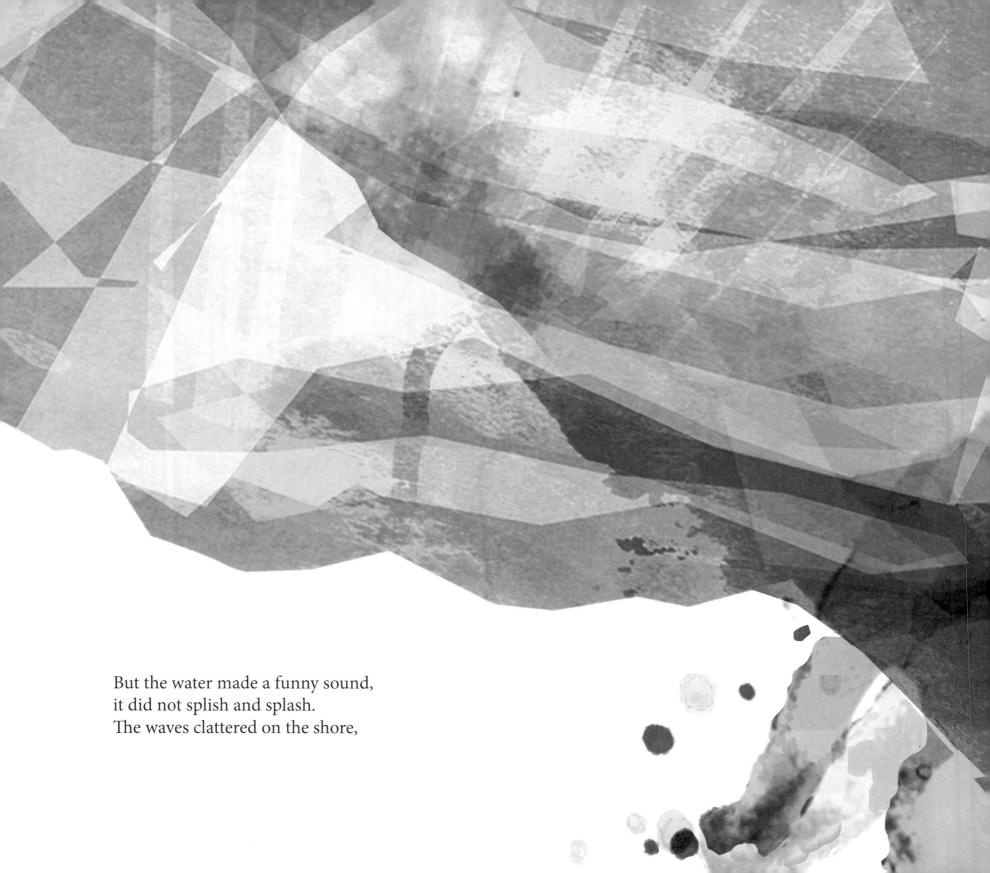

But the water made a funny sound,
it did not splish and splash.
The waves clattered on the shore,

they banged and creaked and crashed.

A dolphin with a bottle nose rode a crackling wave of plastic.
He squeaked, "We once surfed smooth green waves,

they really were fantastic."

"The sand is made of plastic too,"
a pretty mermaid cried.
"Little balls of many colours
brought here by the tide."

The turtle met some cranky crabs with shiny, see-through shells
that crackled as they scurried and had writing on as well.

A pink shark swam through plastic bags
floating in the ocean.
A seahorse stuck his head out
of a tube of suntan lotion.

"What a mess!" said Turtle,
"What is all this plastic for?"
"For toys and bottles," squawked a bird,
"for crisp packets and straws."

"Cotton buds and bottle tops cover the ocean floor.
The people made too many, then made more and more!"

crisps

"Action stations,"

Turtle cried, "we have to make a plan.
Our planet needs us all to make it better if we can."
The turtle looked far out to sea and had a big idea.
"I'm off to change the world," he said, "I'll fix this, have no fear."

"How can you?" laughed his friends.
"You're just a small thing with a shell."
"I may be small, but small things can do

great big things as well!"

The turtle jumped into the sea, his heart was full of pride.
The bird flew low above him, his friends swam by his side.

The crabs with plastic armour,
the whales with plastic bellies,
the mermaids crying plastic tears,
the fish, the rays, the jellies.

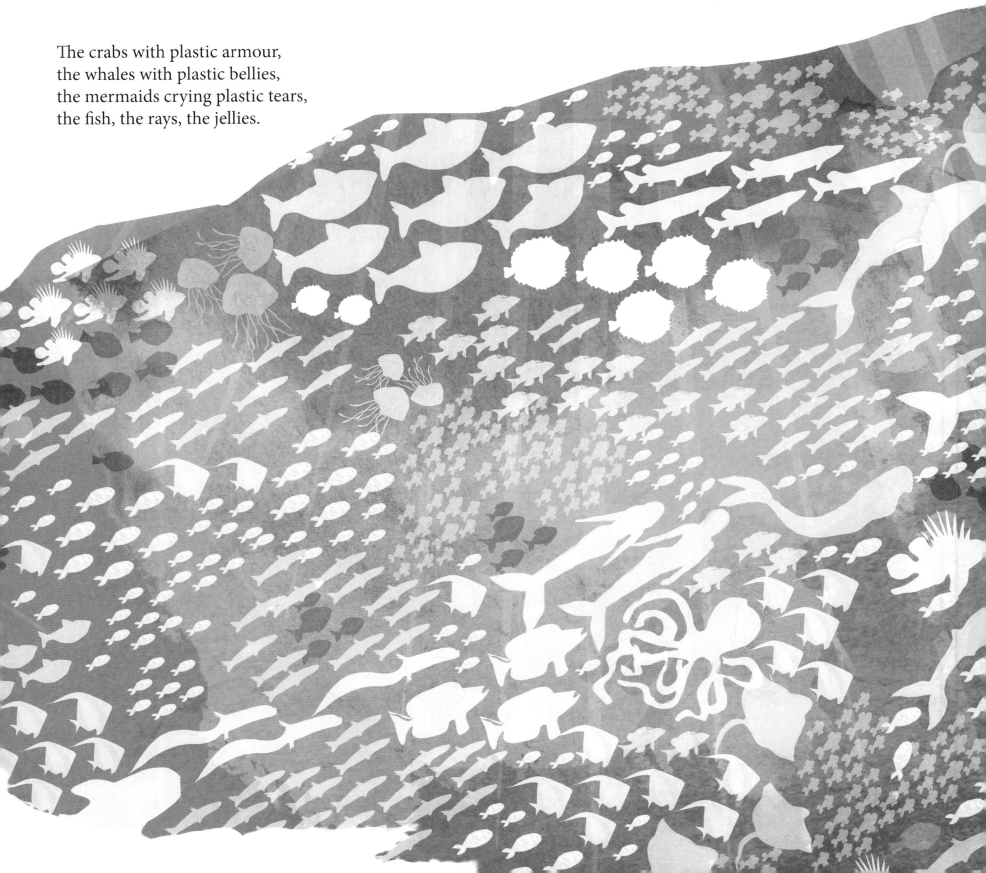

The seahorse and an octopus,
the clams with plastic shells.
As they travelled through the ocean,
many others came as well.

They spread their message to the world, to places far and wide.

They found a mini army to help them turn the tide.

The turtle asked the children, "Please pass this message on:
we have to save our oceans, or the fish will all be gone!

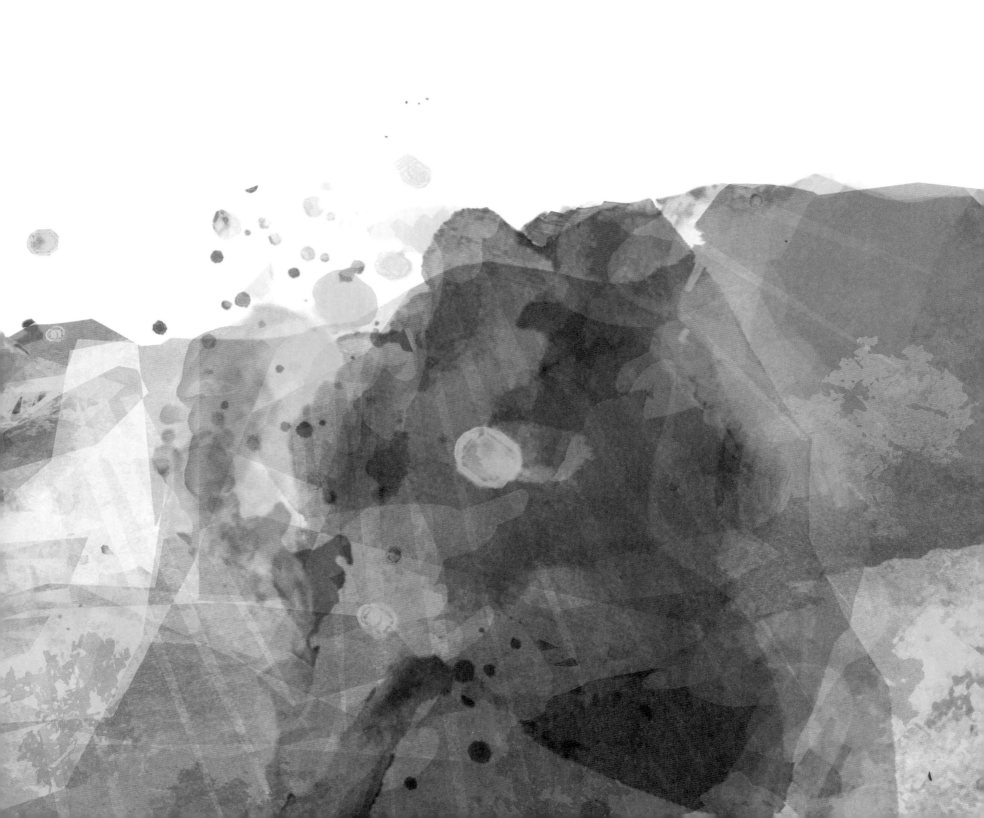

"Use paper straws, paper bags, a toothbrush of bamboo.
Fill a bottle from the tap, don't flush wipes down the loo!

"All bananas have a skin,
they don't need plastic wrapping.
Pick up litter from the beach
and we will all be clapping.

"All bananas have a skin,
they don't need plastic wrapping.
Pick up litter from the beach
and we will all be clapping.

"Every tiny change we make will add up with the others.
Ask your friends to help you, your sisters and your brothers."

So if you want to keep our planet beautiful and clean,
and help the creatures save their homes, remember what you've seen.

We all can make a difference, be you big, small, boy, or girl.

Reduce, reuse, recycle. Be a hero!

Save the world!